OLIVIA™
and Her Alien Brother

adapted by Maggie Testa
based on the screenplay written
by Jill Gorey and Barbara Herndon

illustrated by Patrick Spaziante

Simon Spotlight
New York   London   Toronto   Sydney   New Delhi

Based on the TV series OLIVIA™ as seen on Nickelodeon™

SIMON SPOTLIGHT
An imprint of Simon & Schuster Children's Publishing Division
1230 Avenue of the Americas, New York, New York 10020
OLIVIA™ Ian Falconer Ink Unlimited, Inc. and © 2014 Ian Falconer and Classic Media, LLC
All rights reserved, including the right of reproduction in whole or in part in any form.
SIMON SPOTLIGHT and colophon are registered trademarks of Simon & Schuster, Inc.
For information about special discounts for bulk purchases, please contact Simon & Schuster Special Sales at 1-866-506-1949
or business@simonandschuster.com.
Manufactured in the United States of America 1213 LAK
First Edition 10 9 8 7 6 5 4 3 2 1
ISBN 978-1-4424-9749-8
ISBN 978-1-4424-9750-4 (eBook)

"Look what I made with my pancake," Ian announced one morning at breakfast. "It's a picture of Olivia."
Olivia said, "That doesn't look like me. That looks like a space alien."
"Take me to your leader," replied Ian in his best alien voice.
Olivia began adding her own touches to her pancake portrait. "No great pancake portrait is complete without bows," she explained.

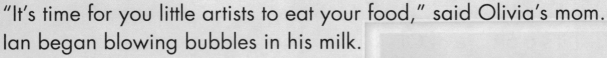

"It's time for you little artists to eat your food," said Olivia's mom.
Ian began blowing bubbles in his milk.
"Mom, are you sure Ian is a member of our family?" Olivia asked.

"Yes, sweetie. I'm positive," her mom replied.
"Because he acts like he's from another planet," added Olivia.
"Another planet?" Olivia's dad chimed in. "I was just reading about a new exhibit at the planetarium. It sounds like it's out of this world!"
"Let's go," Olivia's mom suggested. "We can have a family outing."

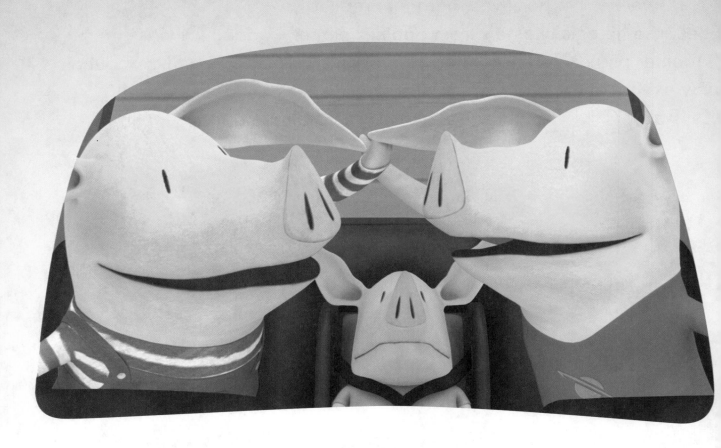

After breakfast Olivia and her family piled into the car. Olivia scratched her ears. Ian scratched his ears. Olivia leaned against the front seat. Ian leaned against the front seat.

"Stop it!" Olivia told him.

"Ian, Olivia, settle down," their mom called from the front seat.

"I didn't do anything," protested Olivia.

"I didn't say anything," added Ian.

Olivia's dad had an idea. "Let's see who can be quiet the longest!"

Olivia and Ian both stopped talking, but then they started making faces at each other. Baby William began to cry.

"You made William cry," Ian told Olivia.

"Ha!" said Olivia gleefully. "You talked first."

Soon they arrived at the planetarium. There was so much to see! Olivia and Ian especially loved the glow-in-the-dark planet mobiles.

"If I had glow-in-the-dark planets in my room, I'd probably go to bed early every night, just so I could look at them," Olivia told her mother. But Olivia's mom shook her head. "No glow-in-the-dark planets today, sweetie."

Olivia sighed. "Well, at least I won't have to go to bed early now, but I

Later Ian looked through the telescope to see if he could spot any planets. "Did you know Pluto is not a planet anymore? And Mercury is the hottest planet in the solar system?" Ian asked his family.

How does Ian know all of this? Olivia wondered. *Maybe he's an alien!*

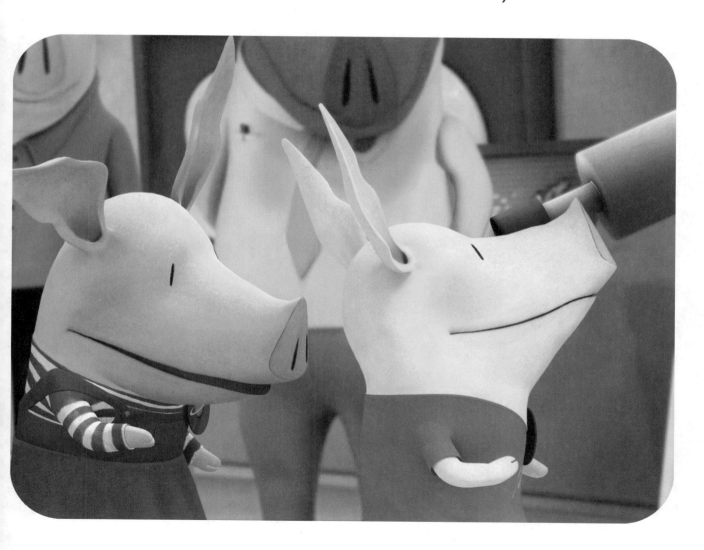

On the ride home, Olivia imagined what Ian
the alien looked like.
"Beep, beep, blurg," says Ian the alien.
"Who are you?" Olivia asks him.
"Who are you?" Ian the alien repeats.

"Mom, Ian's an alien from outer space!" cried Olivia.
"It's not polite to call your brother names, sweetheart," replied Olivia's mom.

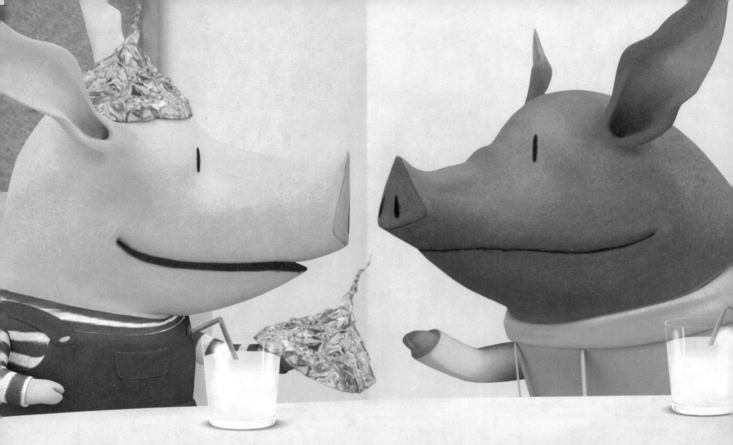

Back at home Olivia told Julian what she'd discovered about Ian.
"Guess what? Ian is an alien from outer space!" she began. "It's
obvious he's studying intelligent life forms on earth."
Then they heard Ian running toward them.
"Quick, we need to put these on," Olivia instructed, handing Julian a
hat made out of tinfoil.
"What are they?" asked Julian.
"Alien mind blockers," answered Olivia. "We don't want him to know
what we're thinking."

Ian ran into the room with Perry. They were both wearing metal bowls on their heads. They stared at Olivia and Julian but didn't say anything. Then they left the room.

"See, I told you he's from outer space," said Olivia.

"What about Perry?" asked Julian.

"He's probably using Perry's special doggy hearing to help him communicate with his home planet," Olivia replied.

Julian nodded. "It's all starting to make sense."

Olivia and Julian followed Ian up to his room. Olivia tried peering through the peephole to see what her alien brother was doing. "Go away, earthling," Ian said in his alien voice. "Annoying older sisters are not allowed."
"What do you think he's doing in there?" asked Julian.

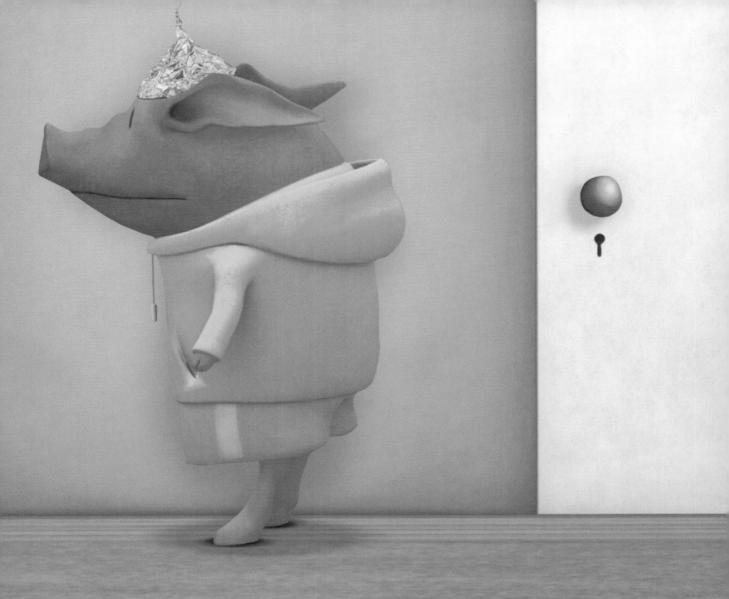

"Probably building something to rid the world of older sisters," replied Olivia. "I have to find out what that space-alien-pretending-to-be-my-brother is up to!"

So Olivia waited and waited and then waited some more for Ian to come out of his room. Soon it was time for Julian to leave, and still Olivia waited. After a while Olivia fell asleep and Ian finally came out of his room. He was holding a box.

Olivia woke up and began to chase him.
"Ian, come back here," she yelled.
"No," said Ian. "It's not ready yet."
"What's not ready yet?" asked Olivia.

As Olivia chased Ian around the house, she imagined that she was an adventurer chasing an alien through outer space.

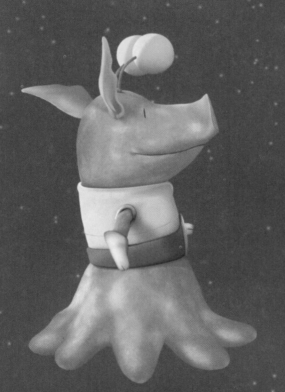
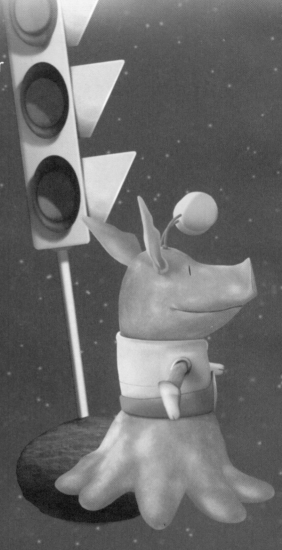

Space adventurer Olivia dodges asteroids and comets as she follows Ian the alien. Ian the alien zooms away just as the outer space traffic light turns red.

Space adventurer Olivia has to wait as aliens cross the intergalactic highway.
"Please hurry," space adventurer Olivia pleads with them. "My alien brother is getting away."

Soon Olivia had chased Ian all the way back to his room. She was just about to catch him when she landed on his skateboard and coasted into the closet. Ian closed the door. Olivia was trapped by her space alien brother!

"What do you plan to do with me, space alien?" Olivia called from inside the closet.
"Quiet, earthling, or else," warned Ian.
"Or else what?" asked Olivia.

Ian went into the closet and handed the box to Olivia. "Or else I'll give you this." Olivia opened the box. "Glow-in-the-dark planets?"

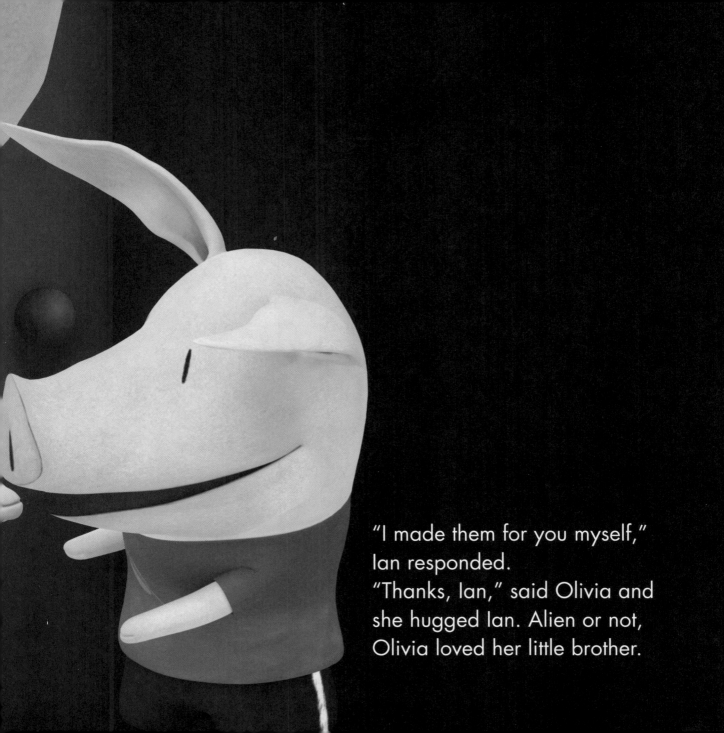

"I made them for you myself," Ian responded.
"Thanks, Ian," said Olivia and she hugged Ian. Alien or not, Olivia loved her little brother.

Later that night Olivia's dad hung her
glow-in-the-dark planet mobile from her ceiling.
"Ian's design is really quite inventive.
You have to admire his creativity," he said.
"You're right," Olivia agreed. "Maybe having
an alien for a brother isn't so bad after all."
"Alien?" asked Olivia's dad.
But Olivia was already asleep.